To my mother, Nellie Bullock Franklin

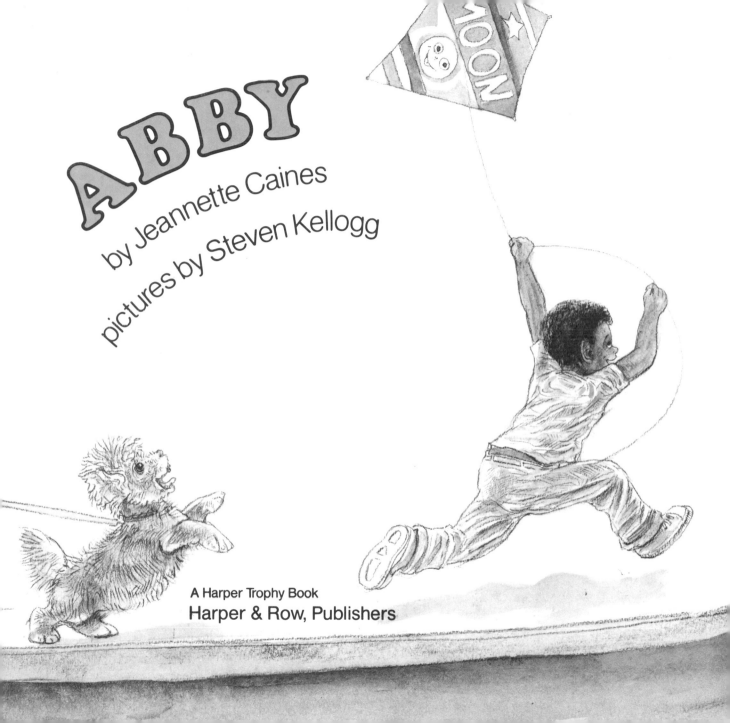

ABBY

by Jeannette Caines

pictures by Steven Kellogg

A Harper Trophy Book
Harper & Row, Publishers

Library of Congress Catalog Card Number: 73–5480
Trade ISBN 0–06–020921–6
Harpercrest ISBN 0–06–020922–4
Trophy ISBN 0–06–443049–9
First Harper Trophy edition, 1984.

Abby? Abby, where are you?

Looking at my baby book.

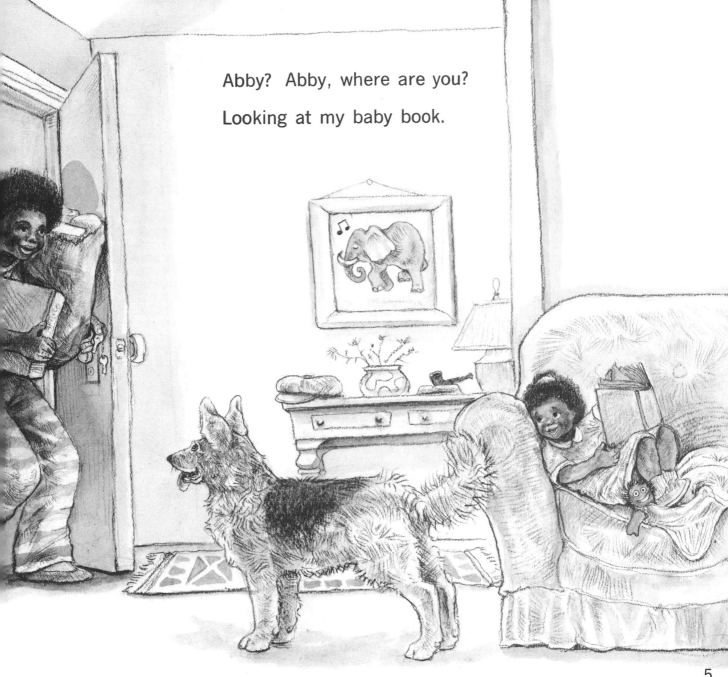

Ma, where did I come from?

Manhattan.

How old was I when you and Daddy got me?

Eleven months and thirteen days.

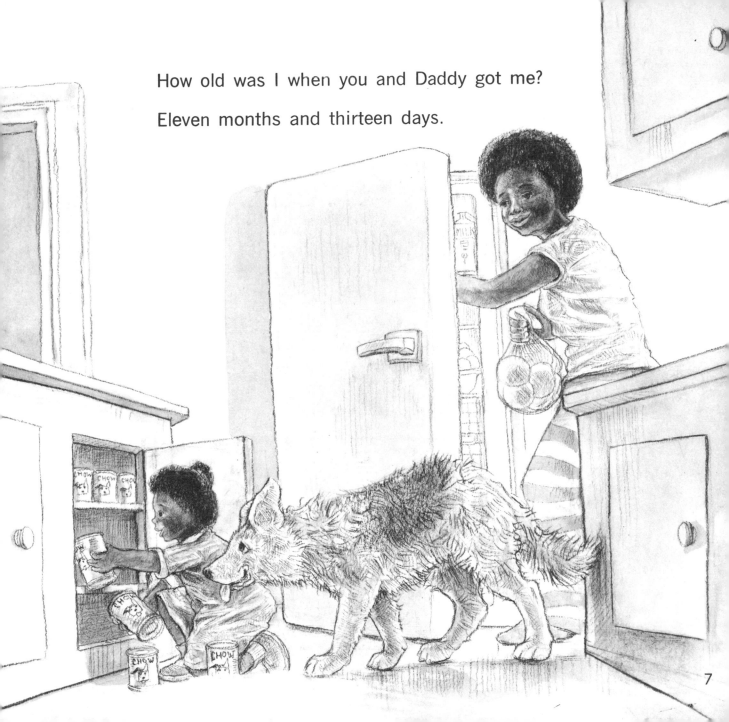

What did I have on?

The pink dress you have on your doll now,
white shoes, and a blue coat with a hood.

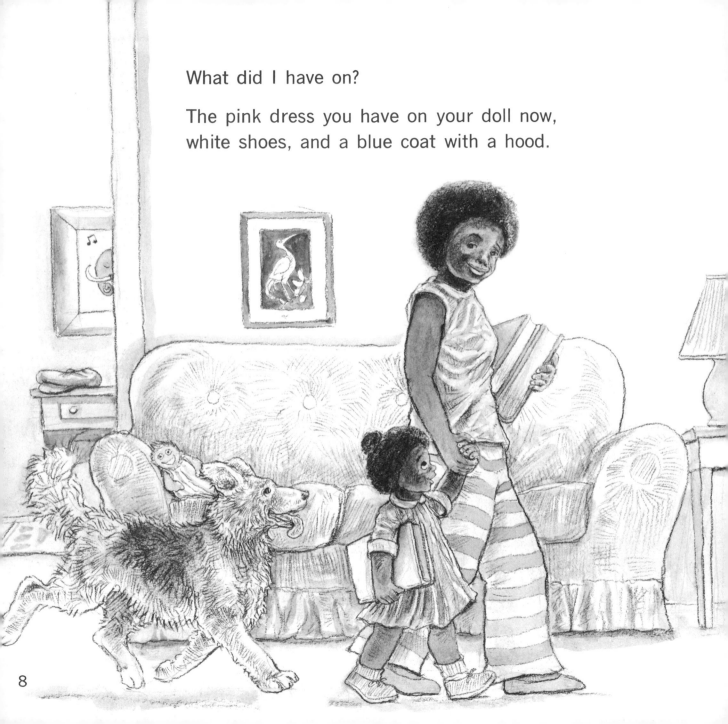

Come, Abby, lunch time
and Kevin will be here in no time flat.

Can I bring my book?

If you don't get any food on it.

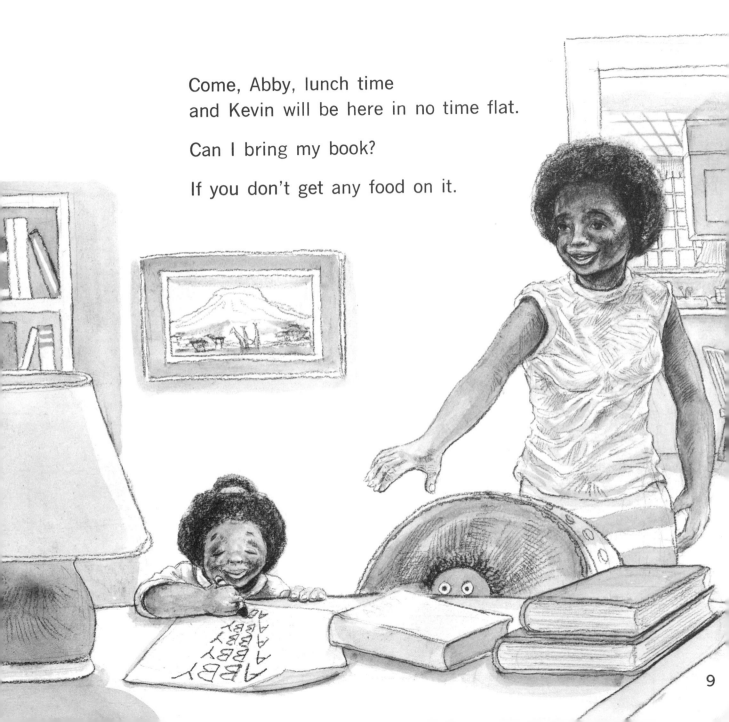

Kevin, is that you?

Yes, what's for lunch?

Kevin, you want to look at my baby pictures?

No, I don't have time.

Kevin, what did you say when you first saw me?

Oh, Abby! I don't know.

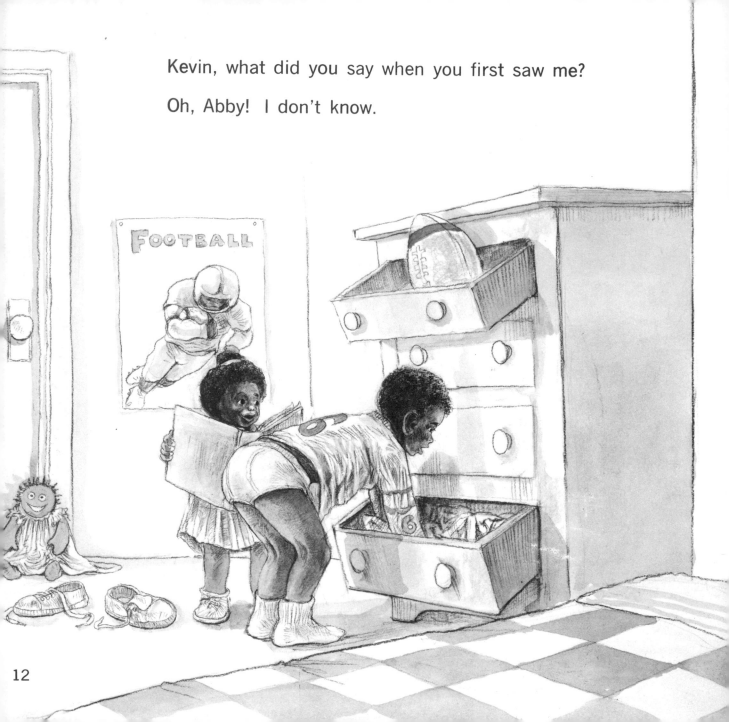

Yes you do. Here it is and you can read it to me.

I don't have time.

I will read it. Kevin said, "Ugh, a girl."

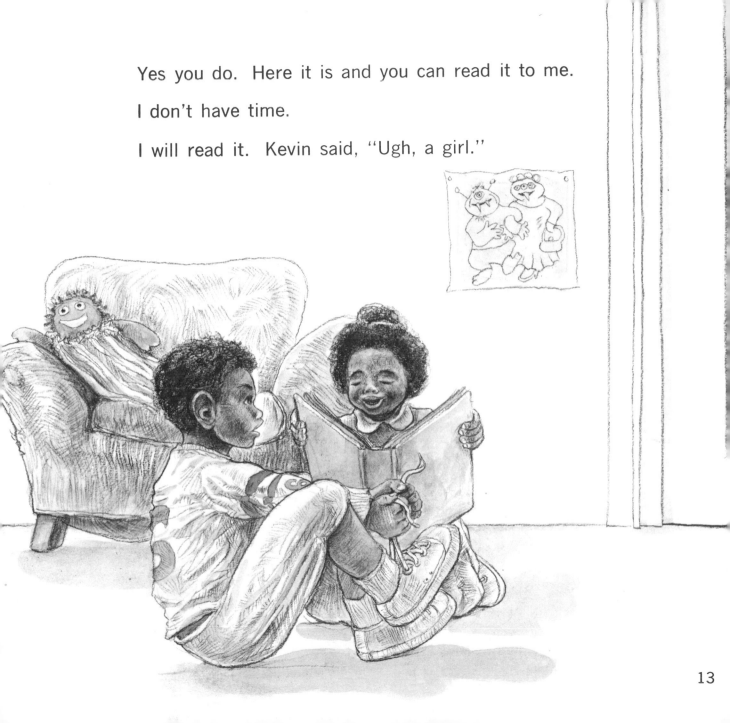

13

Don't you like girls?

No, no, no!

I'm a boy, Kevin.

No, you're a girl. I'm a boy.

No, you're a girl.

Why she always gotta cry like that?

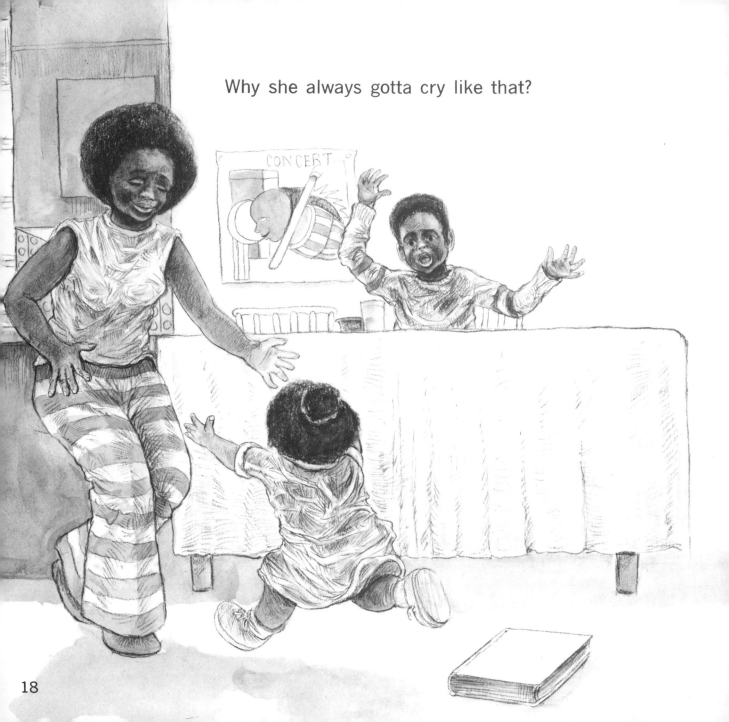

Kevin, Abby loves you
and she thinks you don't like her because she's a girl.

Okay, girl, I like you.

I'm a g-i-r-l!

Okay, okay, I'll read one page.

YOUR FIRST VISITORS.

I know, I know—Grandma Nellie.

YOUR FIRST WORDS.

Bottle.

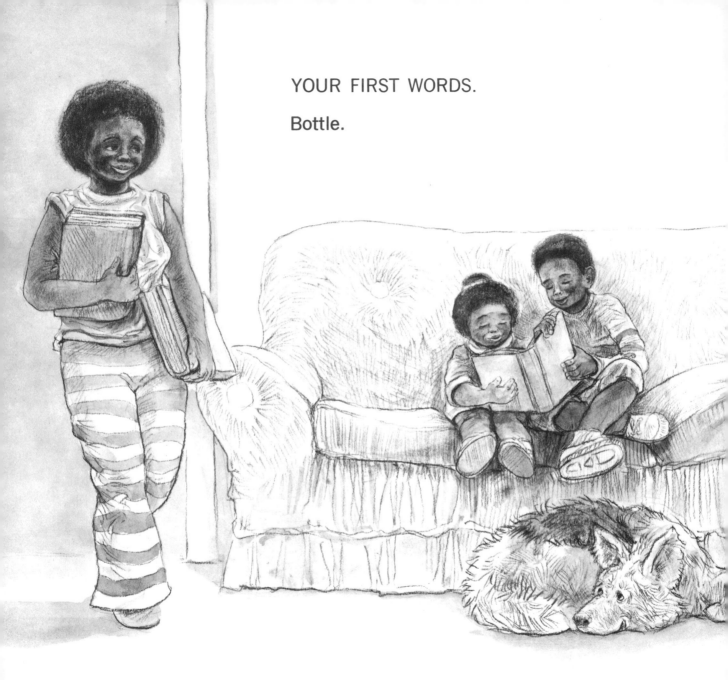

Ma, can I bring Abby for show-and-tell next week? Miss Paige said it's okay.

What are you going to tell about me?

That you're adopted, that we get to keep you
forever, and I gave you my fire engine
for your birthday. Ma, can I?

We'll see.

I'm going now.

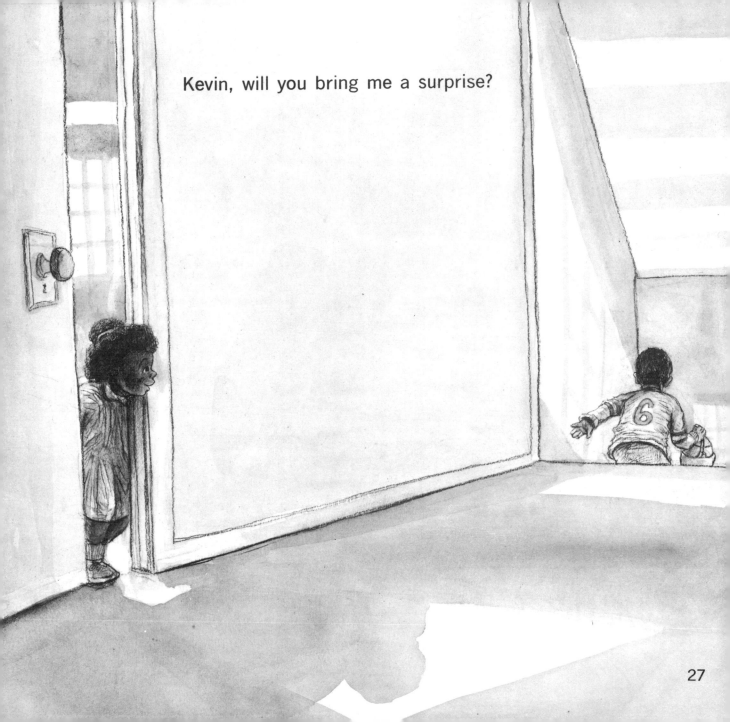

Kevin, will you bring me a surprise?

If you find my turtle stamp.

Was Kevin adopted too?

No.

Let's adopt a boy for Kevin
and I'll save my crib and pillow for him.

We'll talk about it with Daddy
when he comes home tonight.